The Little
Snowflake

Written by
michelle kasim

AuthorHouse™
1663 Liberty Drive
Bloomington, IN 47403
www.authorhouse.com
Phone: 1 (800) 839-8640

This book is printed on acid-free paper.

ISBN: 978-1-7283-4297-9 (sc)
ISBN: 978-1-7283-4445-4 (hc)
ISBN: 978-1-7283-4296-2 (e)

Library of Congress Control Number: 2020901268

Print information available on the last page.

Published by AuthorHouse 01/28/2020

author HOUSE®

For Mom and Dad

The weather started to get cold
trees once lush looked rather old.

A windy burst with frozen breaths,
made it known that autumn has left.

Little critters bury their nuts,
knowing that winter is coming
as the wind begins to gust.

Old mister winter waved
a magical wand,
spreading gentle flakes
from here and beyond.

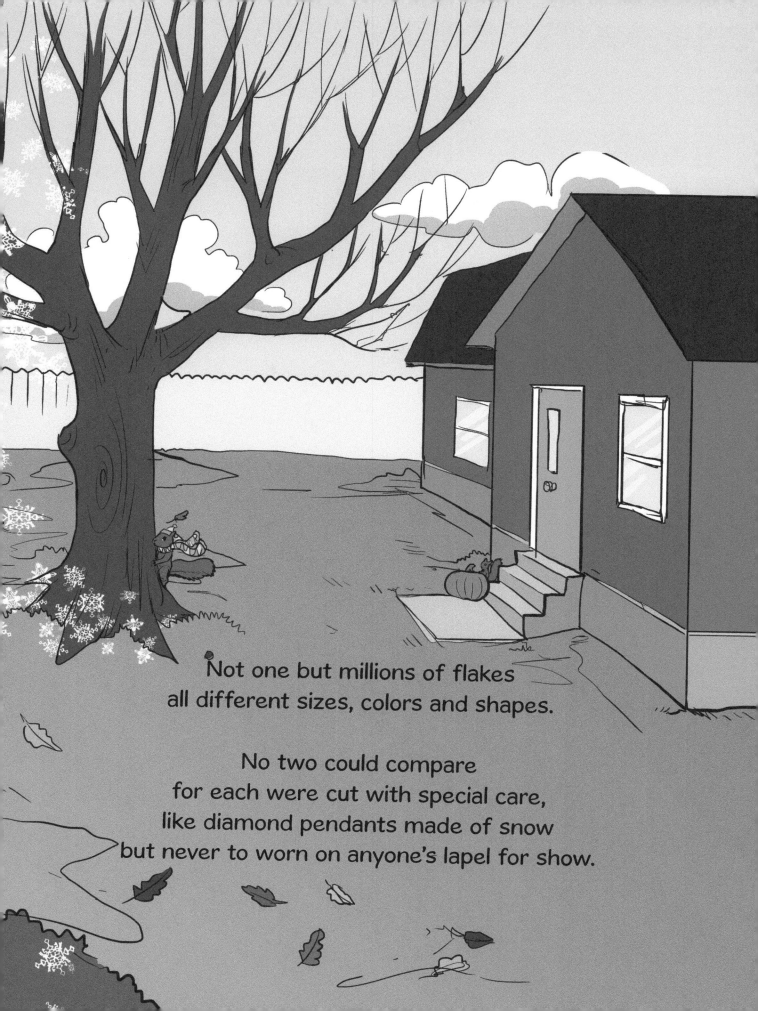

Not one but millions of flakes
all different sizes, colors and shapes.

No two could compare
for each were cut with special care,
like diamond pendants made of snow
but never to worn on anyone's lapel for show.

That is the day Sean found his flake,
such wonder he had to
see such a shape.

It twinkled. It shined with utter grace
that he vowed to keep
it all for himself,
capturing it on his window shelf.

He watched from inside to
keep from the chill.

His snowflake shined so bright like a
special twinkling light in the night.

Sean told his mother of his plan, she

just smiled and said, "It is not meant

to be kept on a window shelf"

and went on to add," Mother Nature

creates such beauty for all to share,"

with this she tucked him in,

laying kisses on his fore head,

his nose and his little chin.

That night, Sean slept
peacefully without a care.

The weather started to warm up

so snow that lay won't last

too long with such warm air.

The rain tapped against his windowpane

lasting until morning

when the sun finally came.

As sun rays streamed through his window,

He awoke and hurriedly made his
way to greet his twinkling friend
only to discover his snowflake
was gone without a trace.

He realized that his mother was right,
such twinkle shine and utter grace
could not be kept in just one place.

after a moment this made him smile...
and he smiled for quite a while.

Author Biography

Michelle was born and raised in New York, but spent many years living in California. It is during her time in California that she became a mother. Her son Sean was the inspiration for the "The Little Snowflake." Originally it was written as a poem so that Sean might understand the joy it is for a child to experience the first snow and the hard lesson when a child realizes that it cannot last forever.

Michelle now lives in Stratford Connecticut with her husband Rameez and their two Yorkshire Terriors Jack and Winnie. Sean is grown and living in California. He continues to inspire his mother to write.

Lightning Source UK Ltd.
Milton Keynes UK
UKHW05073625020
359240UK00009B/216